For Laura, forever a friend

WORCESTERSHIRE COUNTY COUNCIL	
578	
Bertrams	18.02.08
	£4.99
MX	

FELICITY WISHES

Felicity Wishes © 2000 Emma Thomson
Licensed by White Lion Publishing

Text and Illustrations © 2007 Emma Thomson

First published in Great Britain in 2007 by Hodder Children's Books

2

A Catalogue record for this book is available from the British Library.

ISBN: 978 0 340 94398 4

Printed and bound in China.

The paper and board used in this paperback by Hodder Children's Books are natural recyclable products made from wood grown in sustainable forests. The manufacturing processes conform to the environmental regulations of the country of origin.

Hodder Children's Books
A division of Hachette Children's Books, 338 Euston Road, London NW1 3BH
An Hachette Livre UK Company

Emma Thomson's

Felicity Wishes®

Snowy Showdown

and other stories

*Hodder
Children's
Books*

A division of Hachette Children's Books

How to make your Felicity wishes

W I S H

With this book comes an extra-special wish
for you and your best friend.
Hold the book together at each end and
both close your eyes.
Wriggle your noses and think of a
number under ten.
Open your eyes, whisper the numbers you
thought of to each other.
Add these numbers together. This is your

Magic Number.

you

best friend

Place your little finger
on the stars, and say your magic number
out loud together. Now make your wish
quietly to yourselves. And maybe, one day,
your wish might just come true.

Love felicity x

CONTENTS

Snowy Showdown

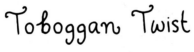

Toboggan Twist

Winter Warmer

Snowy Showdown

Super Whizzer

Snowy Showdown

It was the first day of the Christmas holidays! Felicity Wishes and her fairy friends had made their mince pies, wrapped their presents, hung their decorations and delivered their cards – all ahead of time, and for one extra-special reason. This year, the Grand Winter Sports were coming to Bloomfield!

The Sports were renowned in Fairy World for being the next best thing to the Fairy Winter Olympics. Although the competition wasn't going to start for another day, Felicity and her friends had decided to go to Bloomfield in advance. That way, they could find their way around the grounds, discover where the best seats were and get some sport-celebrities' autographs to save them time when the games began.

"I hope we get to see Jeane Tovell on the skating rink – she looked wonderful on TV last year," said Daisy dreamily as she settled into her seat at the back of the coach taking them to Bloomfield.

"I just can't wait to see the ice hockey!" called Winnie, swishing her arms in the aisle and hitting an invisible puck with her imaginary hockey stick!

Nothing could have prepared the

fairies for what they saw as the coach pulled into the sports grounds. Everything in sight was covered in heaps and heaps of glistening, brilliantly white snow.

"Wow!" Holly sighed. "I've never seen so much snow in my life!"

"It's specially imported in refrigerated trucks from Snow Pole!" said Polly, reading from a programme she had just picked up at the entrance gates.

Everything looked absolutely magical. The white circus-style tents were glistening, the glass-sided arenas were spotless and the loudspeaker system was playing jingling festive music.

 15

"Come on, let's explore!" said
Winnie, peering into one of the tents.

First stop was the ice rink where a practice game of ice hockey was in full swing.

"Yes!" Winnie cheered as the blue team scored.

"Who was that?" Holly asked, confused as to which teams were playing.

"I have no idea!" Winnie replied, not taking her eyes off the game for a second!

Next, the fairies went to see the construction tent.

"What on earth happens in here?" Daisy asked as they fluttered in to have a look. Inside were twenty huge heaps of snow, surrounded by hundreds of seats.

"It's for the snowfairy-building contest!" read Polly from her booklet.

After visiting a second skating rink, several ski slopes, and stopping for warming hot chocolate, the fairies came to the toboggan course.

"Sledging is my favourite winter activity!" cried Daisy.

"It's not exactly sledging, Daisy," Felicity told her friend. "It's a lot more complicated than that, you see…" But before Felicity could finish, her friends had been distracted by a stand selling roasted chestnuts.

Felicity, who loved tobogganing more than any other winter sport, went to look at the course. Just by the starting gate was a large board showing the track. The curves and bends, slopes and dips all looked very exciting to Felicity, and she closed her eyes to imagine herself

 20

hurtling along at top speed! When she opened her eyes again, she noticed a fairy just beyond the starting gate at the top of the track, kneeling down next to a toboggan.

Felicity jumped up and down in excitement. She was desperate to meet one of the participants!

START

TOBOGGAN COURSE

 21

The fairy had her back to Felicity, so Felicity coughed gently to try and get her attention. The fairy was obviously concentrating very hard on what she was doing, because she didn't turn around. Felicity took a few steps closer and coughed again. This time the fairy jumped up so quickly she dropped the small velvet pouch she had been holding, and went a very deep shade of pink.

"I'm so sorry, I didn't mean to startle you," said Felicity, bending to pick the pouch up. But the fairy beat her to it and hastily stuffed it into her pocket.

"No, no, that's OK," she stammered, "I was just, erm, checking the toboggan for any, erm, defects before I have another practice run."

"Oh, wow, so you are a competitor,"

Felicity gushed. "I'm Felicity Wishes, it's so nice to meet you. I absolutely love watching the toboggan racing!"

The fairy smiled. "I'm Tallulah – my friends call me Tally. It's lovely to meet you too, Felicity. But I really must get back to practising now." With that she turned back to her toboggan, checked the time on the large clock hanging overhead, lowered the visor on her crash helmet and began running with the toboggan until she reached the start line, where she jumped in! Felicity watched from her brilliant viewpoint as Tally careered down the course, so fast she was almost a blur!

Felicity fluttered to the bottom of the track in time to see the toboggan finish.

"That was amazing!" Felicity clapped

as Tally clambered out. "How do you do it?"

Again Tally blushed a deep shade of pink. "I, erm, practise, all the time."

"Yes, but how do you make the toboggan go so fast?" Felicity continued questioning. "It's just amazing!"

And then the most unexpected thing happened. The fairy standing in front of Felicity burst into tears.

Felicity instinctively put her arm around Tally's shoulder. "Oh, please don't cry! I'm sorry, I was just curious." Felicity wondered what she had said to upset Tally so much.

"It's not your fault," Tally sobbed. "I'm just so exhausted, I never stop practising, and I've got to beat my record time, it's the only thing I can

 24

do, I haven't got a choice, but it's just wrong and if you saw me doing it then surely other fairies will and..." Tally was sobbing so much that Felicity couldn't make sense of what she was saying.

"Shh, slow down and take a deep breath," Felicity comforted her.

Tally turned to look at Felicity. "I've been cheating!" she said, tears streaming down her face. Then without another word she flew off to a small log cabin nearby, which had "PRIVATE" written above the door.

Felicity followed her in to find tables full of food and drinks and large, comfy sofas in front of big televisions and piles of books. It was obviously the area in which the competitors relaxed before or after their events. Tally was curled up on one of the sofas, still sobbing uncontrollably.

"Don't cry," Felicity said, sitting next to her. "I'm sure we can work it out."

Tally looked at Felicity and now that she had removed her crash helmet

Felicity could see the large dark circles under her eyes. She looked like she hadn't slept for weeks.

"I just can't do it any more," Tally said, blowing her nose. "The fairies who sponsor me are relying on me to win and I've had such brilliant results in the past I can't let them down, but the more I practise the more tired I get, and the more tired I get the slower I am. I just don't know what else to do, so I've been putting sparkle-dust on the runners of my toboggan to make it go faster. That's what I was doing when you came up to me."

Tally, who had stopped crying as she was speaking, burst into fresh tears.

Felicity felt very sorry for her. She was obviously putting herself under a lot of pressure to win, but Felicity

knew that cheating was wrong and against all the sporting rules.

"The important thing is that you've told someone now, before the actual race. As long as you don't cheat on the day—"

Before Felicity could finish, Tally interrupted her. "But that's the thing.

I have to cheat or I won't win!" Tally howled.

"You've won in the past without cheating, so you can do it again!" Felicity said encouragingly. "Now, you have to get some rest before tomorrow. Where do you sleep?" Felicity asked, taking charge.

"I've got a bed through there," Tally said, pointing to a door, "but I've not slept for the past few days. I've been too busy practising."

"You can't win tomorrow unless you've got all your energy, and for that you must sleep!" With this, Felicity helped Tally up and made sure she got straight into bed.

"I'll come and see you tomorrow morning. Make sure you get plenty of rest before then!" Felicity said as she walked towards the door. But Tally didn't hear her. She was already snoring!

It didn't take Felicity long to find Winnie, Holly, Daisy and Polly, who were still standing by the chestnut stand, warming their cold hands.

Grabbing herself a bag of warm chestnuts, Felicity suggested the fairies make their way back to the bus stop, since it was getting dark.

"What were you doing this afternoon, Felicity?" Winnie asked as they trundled along the paths made in the snow.

"Oh, not much, just chatting to Tally, the toboggan fairy. I met her by the toboggan course, and she was very nervous about the race," Felicity replied, deciding it was best not to tell her friends Tally's secret.

* * *

The next day, Felicity woke with a start and jumped out of bed before the sun had even come up. Tally's race started at nine and she had to be there for her new friend.

Felicity had arranged to meet Polly,

Daisy, Holly and Winnie at the bus stop at half past seven, so they would have plenty of time to get to the grounds.

It was a good job they left so early: the queue at the gates stretched for miles and miles around, and it was quarter to nine before Felicity and the others were finally inside the packed grounds.

"What shall we watch first?" Holly asked as she, Daisy and Winnie crowded around Polly's timetable of events.

But Felicity didn't have time to answer! She had to go and see Tally before her race, and she didn't have long to get there. Without a word, she zoomed off in the direction of the toboggan course.

 32

She expected to find Tally standing with all the other competitors at the start of the course, but couldn't see her anywhere.

"Excuse me, have you seen Tally?" she asked a nervous-looking fairy who was hurriedly putting on her wing shields.

"No. I noticed her bedroom door

 33

was still closed this morning when I left the cabin, but I didn't want to disturb her."

"Thank you!" Felicity said, immediately flying to the cabin and bursting in. Tally's door was still closed and when Felicity knocked there was no response.

"Hello! Hello?" she called as she edged the door open.

There on the bed, lying in exactly the same position she had been in when Felicity left her the afternoon before, was Tally, still snoring!

"Wake up!" Felicity called, looking at her watch. It was five to nine!

Tally groaned. "Urg, what time is it?" she asked as she rubbed her eyes. Then she sat bolt upright in bed. "I've got to practise! I've got to practise!"

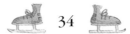

"There's no time!" Felicity said,
pulling the covers back. She tried to
stay as calm as possible, not wanting
to make Tally panic before the race.

 35

"And you've practised enough. It's time for the real thing!"

Felicity helped Tally into her protective clothing as quickly as she could and together they went outside to the start gates.

Luckily Tally wasn't racing first, but she was second and had only a matter of minutes before she had to be standing next to her toboggan at the starting line.

"Just remember, you can only do your best!" Felicity called as Tally went to find her toboggan.

Felicity fluttered to the finish line, where Holly, Polly, Daisy and Winnie were standing. As she flew, Felicity shut her eyes tight for a second and wished with all her heart that Tally would do well in the race.

She arrived just in time to see Tally zoom towards the end. The crowds were cheering and the commentators' voices were booming excitedly over the speaker system. But Felicity didn't hear a thing they were saying as she rushed over to Tally, who was climbing out of her toboggan.

"You were fantastic!" Felicity gushed, hugging her.

"But I didn't use sparkledust, so it can't have been fast enough," Tally worried.

But something caught Felicity's attention and for a second she stopped listening to Tally.

"…in record time! No one has ever been down this course so fast before, and I doubt anyone will beat this time today!" the commentator

 37

fairy was saying to the crowds.

"You did it!" Felicity screamed. "All by yourself."

Tally beamed. With the help of her new friend she had learnt an important lesson: all you need to do is believe in yourself, and anything is possible.

Anything is possible

with the help of your friends

Toboggan Twist

Toboggan Twist

Felicity Wishes and her friends Holly,
Polly, Winnie and Daisy had spent the
entire day at the Grand Winter Sports
in Bloomfield, watching ice skating,
snowfairy-building, skiing, several ice
hockey matches and, most importantly,
tobogganing.

Tobogganing was Felicity's favourite
winter sport – and not only had she
watched the race, but she had helped
Tally the toboggan fairy to win!

"I can't thank you enough, Felicity,"

Tally said again. She hadn't stopped thanking Felicity all afternoon!

Now all the fairies were sitting around a blazing log fire, munching on marshmallows and sipping hot chocolate in Tally's log cabin.

"Really, you don't have to keep thanking me!" Felicity smiled. "I'm just glad you won!"

Poor Tally had felt under so much pressure to win the race that she had been cheating in her practice laps. Luckily, Felicity had seen her just in time and managed to persuade Tally that she could win by herself – all she had to do was believe.

"Yes, but if it wasn't for you I might have cheated in the final race, and then I'd have been disqualified and I might never have been able to race again!" Tally gushed. "If only there was some way I could show you how grateful I am…"

Tally fell quiet and started to think.

"No, you don't have to! I'm happy to know—" But before Felicity could finish her sentence, Tally jumped up from the beanbag she'd been sitting on.

"I know!" she cried, a huge smile on her face. "Come to the Fairy Winter Olympics with me!"

Felicity was shocked at Tally's kind offer. The Grand Winter Sports were tiny compared to the Fairy Winter Olympics.

"Thank you, but it's too generous of you! I really don't want to leave my friends over Christmas, and…" Felicity couldn't think of another reason not to go.

"I'm not taking no for an answer!" Tally said, as she flung her arms

 46

around Felicity. "The race is on Christmas Eve, so all your friends can join us for the celebrations. Anyway, you'd be doing me a favour! I need you there as my good luck charm. I won't be able to win without you!"

Felicity glanced at her friends to see that they were all smiling at her, excitement twinkling in their eyes.

"Well, OK then!" Felicity said, returning Tally's hug. "But I'm not your good luck charm. You'd be brilliant without me – I'm just coming along to watch!"

* * *

Felicity only had a few days to pack before she left for Snow Pole.

"Make sure you take plenty of scarves, gloves and hats," Polly advised her. "And several thick jumpers. Snow

Pole is the coldest place in Fairy World."

"I heard that at the Olympics they have magical hovering heaters that follow you around wherever you go," said Daisy.

"Think of all the Olympic stars you'll meet!" said Holly dreamily.

"Make sure you take plenty of

photos," Winnie instructed Felicity. "We don't want to miss a thing!"

"But most importantly," Polly said with a stern face, "have fun!"

Felicity smiled at her friends. She couldn't wait until they joined her on Christmas Eve.

"The only thing is…" she said carefully, packing an extra hat into her case, "I'm worried that Tally is going to think she can't win without me. As much as I want to go, she mustn't think I'm her good luck charm. She has to realize that she needs to believe in herself."

Polly, the most sensible of Felicity's friends, smiled.

"Why don't you talk to her about it? I'm sure she'll understand."

* * *

 49

Felicity tried to talk to Tally on the flight to Snow Pole, but her friend slept the whole way there and when the plane landed Felicity was too amazed by the scenery to speak.

A thick blanket of pure-white snow covered everything in sight, all the way up to the mountains, circling the grounds where the games were to take place.

And if the mountains themselves looked majestic, their tips hidden behind fluffy white clouds, they were nothing compared to the huge white tents sparkling in the winter sunshine.

* * *

Felicity had been amazed when she'd first seen the Grand Winter Sports grounds in Bloomfield, but they were tiny in comparison!

The tents here were ten times the size, the stadiums could seat thousands more fairies and the snow was spotless.

The gates to the grounds were made of sparkling ice, carved into the most intricate patterns, and either side of the gates stood perfectly smooth igloos for the ticket fairies.

Felicity and Tally immediately went over to show their tickets to a fairy dressed in a stripy pink and white scarf.

"The tents host the less competitive events, and the more serious games are in the stadiums. It's quite a distance to the skiing and tobogganing courses, so it's best to use the chairlifts provided. For shorter distances, frequent horse-drawn carts will circle the grounds.

 51

Wherever you see an igloo, there will
be a fairy inside happy to help you
with any enquiries. The hovering
heaters we have used in the
past melted the snow,
leaving puddles at your
feet, so this year we
have heated blankets
to wrap around
your shoulders."
The fairy handed
them each a
soft blanket.
"Enjoy your
visit!"

"Wow." It was the first word Felicity had managed to say since their arrival.

"I know!" Tally smiled. "Where shall we go first?"

Just then a beautiful wooden cart drove past, painted with gold and red swirls and pulled by a perfectly white horse.

"Quick, it's empty! Let's have a tour!" Tally said, grabbing Felicity's arm and pulling her over to the carriage.

"A tour of the grounds, please, ending at the chairlift to the tobogganing

course!" Tally instructed the horse as
she jumped into the cart.

Felicity and Tally tucked their warm
blankets over their knees and snuggled
into their seats as they began the tour.

Everything was so wonderful Felicity
couldn't take it all in. They passed
fairies skiing down the slopes, fairies
twisting and turning in their sledges,
and fairies enjoying snowball fights.

In what seemed like no time at all,
they reached the chairlift and climbed
into it.

It swung them into the hills to the top
of the tobogganing course - where
Tally's small log cabin
awaited her.

CABINS

Felicity sighed happily as she snuggled down in bed that night. She was missing her friends back in Little Blossoming, though. If only sensible Polly was there, to tell her how to improve Tally's confidence! Felicity couldn't wait until her friends arrived in a couple of days' time.

* * *

Tally was up bright and early the next morning and woke Felicity with a nudge.

"Come on, Felicity, I can't practise without you there as my lucky charm!" Tally called to a bleary-eyed Felicity.

"Ah, yes, about that," Felicity began, but Tally was already outside and warming up.

By the time Felicity was dressed and outside, Tally was standing next to her toboggan, her protective clothing in place, waiting to start.

"Go straight to the end of the course once I'm off," Tally instructed, "just like you did last time I raced."

Luckily for Felicity, the course was circular and ended not far from the start.

As Tally pulled into her finish, Felicity could see the frown on her face.

"It's no good," she said, removing her crash helmet, "you must be too far away from me. I slowed down on the outer edge of the track."

"I really don't think—" Felicity tried again, but Tally interrupted her.

"Perhaps if you fly around the course with me I'd be faster," Tally thought aloud. "Oh no, that's no good, you wouldn't be able to fly as fast as the toboggan. Hmmm…"

"But it's not me!" Felicity insisted.

Tally was in her own world of thought and didn't hear.

"I know!" she said, a smile spreading on her face. "You can come in the toboggan with me. I'll get one with room for two fairies, and safety-wear for you!"

And she flew off, speeding towards the start of the track.

"Oh dear!" Felicity sighed to herself as she fluttered after Tally.

* * *

Felicity tried again and again to tell Tally how she felt, but each time she began Tally interrupted in her excitement. Before Felicity knew it, Tally was pushing a crash helmet on to her head!

"Now, all you have to do is run with the toboggan until we reach the start line, then jump in!" Tally told Felicity as they made their way to the toboggan. "It's very simple. Then just sit behind me and keep your head down and your wings in!"

It took Felicity a few practices to get everything right, but on their third attempt she was tucked in the toboggan in excellent time.

As the toboggan got faster and faster, Felicity loved it more and more. It was so exciting, seeing the mountains pass by in a blur, curving to the left then swinging to the right.

The finish line came far too soon for Felicity, even though the course was the longest in Fairy World. She couldn't wait to get back in to have

 61

another go, and she'd completely forgotten about her lucky-charm worries.

* * *

"My time just keeps getting better and better!" Tally beamed after their fifth lap together. "Obviously it's different having two of us in the toboggan instead of just me, but if I calculate the extra weight against the faster time…"

Felicity didn't quite understand Tally's calculations, but knew that she loved the experience of travelling at top speed.

"Really, all I'm doing is improving your confidence by being there, Tally," she tried to explain.

"Nonsense! You're my lucky fairy!" Tally said. "Come on, let's beat our record time again!"

Felicity put her crash helmet back on, lowered the visor and stood at the back of the toboggan ready to go.

Together Tally and Felicity made a brilliant start, jumping into the toboggan very quickly. As they sped around the first corner, Felicity was sure they were already going faster than they'd been before. They veered to the right and twisted to the left as thick, heavy snowflakes began to fall around them, dancing in front of Felicity's visor until she could barely see a thing.

Felicity knew the course quite well by now and remembered the sharp bend and sudden dip that it took towards the end. The runners had almost come off the ice the last time they practised, and she dreaded to think what would happen now. Just then, she felt a sharp jolt. The toboggan had turned over and was sliding along the snow on its side!

When they eventually came to a halt, Tally clambered out.

"Felicity, are you OK?" she asked, pushing Felicity's visor up for her. "We came off the track where it dips! We're so lucky the soft new snow

 64

broke our fall. Tell me you're not
hurt!"

While Tally had been talking,
Felicity had been trying to get out of
the toboggan by shuffling sideways –
but she just couldn't seem to stand
up!

"Yes, I think I'm OK, nothing hurts,
only, erm, which way is up?" Felicity
knew it sounded like a silly question,
but she had completely lost her
sense of direction.

"Here, let me
help!" Tally
held out
her hand –

 65

but as soon as she had helped Felicity out and stood her up, Felicity fell back over again!

"I can't seem to find my balance," Felicity explained as she rolled around in the snow and started to giggle.

Tally helped Felicity up again and again, but every time she did Felicity just fell over.

"Can you fly?" Tally asked, helping Felicity to struggle out of her wing protectors.

Felicity hovered above the ground, upside down!

Tally immediately called a nurse on her mobile phone for assistance.

"It's just your balance," the nurse explained when she arrived. "You haven't got any major injuries. Rest for a few days and you should be fine."

 66

She smiled and fluttered away.

"Oh no! What am I going to do? I'll never win now!" Tally moaned, sinking to the ground beside Felicity.

"Tally, I've been trying to tell you since you got here. You don't need me!" Felicity told her friend.

"Yes I do, I—"

This time it was Felicity's turn to interrupt.

"No, you don't. You won races before we were friends. I don't bring you luck – our crash proves that. All I do is believe in you, which helps you to believe in yourself, so you win. It's as simple as that!"

Tally looked doubtfully at Felicity. But then she started to remember the very first time she'd won a sledging race, on a make-do tin tray.

"It's true!" she said as she jumped up from the ground, realizing she had a very cold, wet bottom! "There have been times in the past when I've lost races, but it's only made me even more determined to win the next one! I've gone from a tatty old tin tray to the Fairy Winter Olympics, which is something I'd never dreamt would ever happen. Just like a toboggan race – I've had to ride the downhill lows to reach the uphill peaks."

Felicity beamed at Tally's renewed confidence.

"Now I've got to rest. This afternoon I'll practise for the big race. And, yes, I might not win, but I'll do my best!" Tally said, marching off into the snow.

"Urm, Tally, come back!" Felicity called. "Tally!"

 69

Remembering her friend, Tally spun around and quickly fluttered back. "Oops, sorry, Felicity! I forgot you were feeling a bit topsy-turvy!"

Felicity and Tally giggled as they walked back to the cabin. Tally supported Felicity as she tried not to topple upside down, and together they talked about how she could make this next race Tally's best yet – even without a good luck charm!

You don't need
good luck charms

with friends
by your side

Winter Warmer

Winter Warmer

Felicity Wishes was at the Fairy Winter
Olympics! She had shown her new
friend Tally how to believe in herself,
and Tally was now ready for the first
warm-up race that afternoon. And
Felicity was very excited – her friends
Holly, Winne, Polly and Daisy were
arriving that morning!

Felicity and Tally flew to the
entrance gates to meet their friends.

"I've missed you so much!" cried
Felicity, flinging her arms around all

of them. "Come and have a hot chocolate in our cabin!"

The six friends warmed themselves up by the fire and caught up on all the latest gossip. Then they put their outdoor things on, ready for Tally's warm-up race.

"When you told us how cold it was in Snow Pole, Polly insisted that we brought loads of warm clothes with us!" giggled Winnie, wrapping her third scarf round her neck.

"Normally I'd have been helping out the other Christmas Fairies," said Holly, putting one stylish coat on top of another, "but when they heard that I'd had an invitation to the Olympics they wanted me to make the most of it!"

They headed down to the toboggan course.

"How long does each lap take?" Daisy asked, thinking about the nice log fire back in the cabin.

"Oh, it feels like seconds when you're actually racing," Felicity replied, thinking back to Tally's practice laps where she'd been in the back of the toboggan.

"Quick, it's Tally's turn," Polly said. "Think lucky thoughts!"

Felicity and her friends concentrated as hard as they could on hoping and wishing that Tally would win. She hadn't believed she was good enough to win on her own before she had met Felicity, and Felicity really wanted her to win this race by miles.

The fairies gasped in unison as they saw Tally leave the start line.

"She seems to be going very quickly,"

Holly said, staring in
wonder at the
blurred
Tally.

START

"She's
getting
faster and
faster!" Winnie
said excitedly.
"Come on, Tally!"
Daisy shouted.
Felicity watched,
spellbound, as the
toboggan sped around
each corner. She knew
that Tally was going

much faster than she ever had before.

"You know, I think that's a bit too fast!" said Daisy.

Tally was gathering speed so quickly that even the race commentators couldn't keep up with her progress and were starting to look worried.

"I'm not sure that's safe," said Polly.

Felicity bit her lip. She could see that Tally was approaching a difficult dip and closed her eyes, *wishing* as hard as she could that Tally wouldn't crash.

When Felicity opened her eyes again, she couldn't believe what she saw. Tally hadn't crashed at all! Instead, she'd flown straight off the course and was now speeding through the air, still in her toboggan!

The crowds gasped.

 79

"Where's she going?" Holly asked, wide-eyed.

"I don't know!" Felicity replied, squinting as Tally became a smaller and smaller dot in the distance. "But wherever it is, I think we should follow!"

And with that the five fairy friends flew off into the sky, heading towards the mountains.

* * *

"Look, there she goes!" Winnie called to the others behind her.

Quickly they flew up to the peak of the tall, snow-covered mountain. Felicity hovered in the air, trying to spot where Tally had gone. There was her toboggan!

Winnie plunged down to the ground, the others close behind. Tally's toboggan, its nose buried in the deep snow, lay silently where it had crashed.

But there was no sign of Tally.

"Well, she can't be hurt if she has managed to climb out," Polly said.

Felicity wasn't so sure. "What if she

 81

fell out as the toboggan plummeted to the ground?" she worried.

Just then Winnie, who had been walking all around the toboggan, looking for clues, called out to her friends.

"Look!" she said, pointing to the ground.

The other fairies fluttered over to see what she was looking at.

There in the soft white snow were

three sets of footprints, side by side.

"I don't understand," said Felicity. "Tally was the only fairy in the toboggan. Who do the other two sets of footprints belong to?"

"I think I know why she didn't fly," Winnie said, twisting around to peer at her own wings. They were fluttering very slowly in the icy cold and it was extremely hard work to move them at all.

"I think our wings are freezing!" Felicity said to the others, who all looked at their wings. The same thing had happened to all of them.

"Let's follow the prints on foot," said Winnie, marching ahead.

"Shouldn't we go back and get help? I mean, what if Tally's hurt and needs a nurse?" Daisy asked, looking back to the mountain and the way they had come.

"The most important thing is to find her, and soon!" urged Polly, looking up at the sky. "The daylight is fading already!"

* * *

So the fairy friends set off into the snowy landscape.

Just as they each thought they couldn't possibly go any further, they

 84

stumbled over the top of a particularly high snow dune and couldn't believe what they saw ahead.

Each of the fairies gasped.

In the snow in front of them was a beautiful palace, made entirely of ice.

"Wow," Winnie said in awe. In all her travels around Fairy World she had never seen a more magical building.

"Where, what, who?" Holly stammered, too shocked to speak.

"It's amazing." Daisy sighed.

Felicity looked at the ground. The footprints led right up to the glistening front door of the palace. "Tally must be inside!" gasped Felicity.

* * *

Tentatively, the fairies walked up to the beautiful entrance of the palace. It felt very strange not to be able to fly, but none of them could use their wings at all.

Holly lifted her hand up to knock at the enormous ice door. To her surprise it swung open at her gentle touch.

"That's odd!" said Felicity. "It looks

like someone has opened it, but there's no one there."

Winnie peeked around the open door into a vast, glistening, and empty hallway. Ice walls reflected their every move and a strange blue light enveloped them all. Strangest of all, it was toastily warm inside!

"Hello? Tally? Anyone home?" Felicity called, stepping inside.

One by one, the others followed her.

"Maybe no one's here. I think we should go back—" Daisy began, but Winnie interrupted her.

"Shh! I can hear someone," she said, holding her finger to her lips and listening very intently.

"It sounds like Tally!" Felicity said, recognizing her friend's voice and following it into a room to the right of the hallway.

They peeped around the door to see a room with everything in it carved out of ice. An enormous and beautiful ice chandelier hung from the ceiling, a long silvery ice table sat in the centre of the room, with twelve beautifully carved ice chairs around it. And there at the head of the table was Tally – talking to herself!

* * *

"I have no idea, I just came over the ridge and flew straight into the air. I didn't stop until I crashed!" she was saying enthusiastically.

Felicity and her friends looked at each other worriedly.

"I think Tally must have banged her head when she fell, and she's just a

little confused?" Daisy suggested.

"Or maybe—" Felicity began, but at that second Tally spotted the fairies and jumped up to greet them.

"Felicity!" she beamed, running over to give them each a hug. "How did you find me?"

"We followed your footprints," Felicity replied, looking carefully at Tally's head. She didn't seem to have any lumps or bumps.

"Oh, you are clever!" Tally said, ushering the fairies into the room. "I was just telling everyone what happened. Wasn't it amazing?"

Holly stared at Tally. "Are you feeling OK?" she asked, placing her hand on Tally's forehead to feel if she had a temperature.

"Fine, thank you," Tally replied. "Come and meet my new friends!"

Felicity, Holly, Polly, Winnie and Daisy reluctantly followed her over to the table where Tally started pointing to each chair.

"This is Laora, Trixie, Bella…"

As Tally spoke and Winnie, Holly,

Polly and Daisy looked at each other anxiously, Felicity looked very hard at where Tally was pointing. At first it looked like nothing was there, but as she squinted her eyes she could just about see the outline of a fairy!

The more she concentrated, the clearer the outline became, until she could see a shimmering fairy sitting in front of her, smiling.

"Hello!" said the ice fairy in a faint voice.

"Ah!" Holly, Polly, Winnie and Daisy all jumped at the sound.

"No, it's OK! You have to concentrate very hard to see us, and not many fairies take the time," the fairy said airily.

"Oops, I forgot!" Tally said with a giggle. "It took me a while to see them too!"

Squinting and concentrating like Felicity had, Daisy, Winnie, Holly and Polly gradually began to see the beautiful fairies.

"What, who, I mean, how are you?" Holly stuttered.

"We're ice fairies," Laora replied.

"But I've never heard of ice fairies," Polly said, puzzled by what she was seeing.

"That's because no one knows about us!" Laora explained. "Like I said, no one usually takes the time to see us - until today!"

Tally beamed. "They saved my life!" she said. "When the toboggan crashed, I was all alone and so cold. I thought I was being lifted out of the toboggan by invisible magic! But it was the ice fairies that brought me here, warmed me up, and now we're having supper!" Tally pointed to the table.

"Please join us," Laora said.

Two other ice fairies got up and ran to get chairs for Felicity and her friends, who couldn't resist the delicious warm goodies in front of them.

The longer they sat eating and chatting, the clearer the ice fairies' features became. Felicity could see her new friends almost as well as she could see Holly, Polly, Daisy or Winnie.

"A few years ago we decided to take

part in the Fairy Winter Olympics," Laora told the fairies between mouthfuls. "But it didn't go very well. I took part in the ice skating, Trixie decided to ski and Bella built a snow fairy – only no one could see us and every fairy in the stadium started squealing when I stepped on to the ice. All anyone could see was a pair of ice skates!" she finished with a giggle. "None of us competed properly in the end."

Felicity wasn't smiling at all. "That's terrible," she said, looking at Laora.

"The Fairy Winter Olympics is open to all fairies, no matter what they look like or where they're from."

"We don't want to scare other fairies!" said Laora. "Living on our own isn't too bad."

For the rest of the meal Felicity looked thoughtful, and when it was over she took Polly aside for a chat.

"There must be something we can do to help," she whispered to Polly. "The ice fairies shouldn't have to have such lonely lives, just because of how they look."

"I know, I was thinking exactly the same thing," Polly replied.

"So what can we do?" Felicity asked, knowing that Polly was the cleverest of the fairies and always had a solution to every problem.

But this time even Polly didn't have any ideas.

Just then Laora and Holly walked past.

"I really like your scarf," Laora was saying.

"Thank you. I made it myself!" Holly said proudly.

"That's it!" Felicity squealed, jumping up and down.

Holly, Polly, Laora and all the other fairies in the room looked at her questioningly.

"You can borrow our outdoor clothes! If you wear them instead of your ice fairy clothes, then everyone will be able to see you and you can join in the competitions!" Felicity said, beaming at her fairy friends.

"That's very kind, Felicity, but we

couldn't possibly," Laora said sadly. "You'd get too cold."

"No, we wouldn't!" Felicity said, an even bigger smile on her face. "You have Polly to thank for that!"

Polly had made sure that they had worn enough layers to keep them warm throughout the day. Felicity was sure they could spare a few!

"Here!" Holly said, taking off her scarf and draping it around Laora's shoulders. "It suits you!"

Hurriedly, Felicity, Winnie, Polly and Daisy took off some of their layers as well, until every ice fairy had at least two items of clothing.

"If we leave now, we'll be back at the Olympics before it gets dark," said Felicity as she looked out of the enormous icy window. "It's the opening ceremony tonight!"

* * *

In all the excitement Felicity and her friends had forgotten about their frozen wings. But in the warmth of the palace they had defrosted perfectly!

Together Felicity and her friends flew with the ice fairies back over the mountain and into the Olympic grounds. They arrived just as the torch-lit opening procession was beginning.

The crowds of fairies gasped as they saw what looked like scarves, hats, gloves, jumpers and tights flying through the air. But the harder they stared, the clearer the ice fairies became.

Laora and her friends took their place in the opening procession, joined

by Tally, Felicity, Holly, Polly, Winnie
and Daisy.

"There's just one thing I don't
understand," Tally shouted over the
noise of the Christmas music playing
all around them. "How did my
toboggan fly?"

"I think maybe I wished a little too

hard!" Felicity giggled, giving her friend a hug.

Meanwhile, Laora and the other ice fairies could be seen more easily than ever before. Their cheeks were glowing with joy. "Thank you so much, Felicity!" Laora cried, as the wintery fireworks began.

Felicity was bursting with happiness. She liked nothing better than to help her friends.

You can be
anything you want

if you really believe
in yourself

Emma Thomson's

felicity Wishes

The Fairy Circus has come

to Little Blossoming in

Perfect Ponies

Perfect Ponies

The Fairy Circus had come to Little Blossoming! Felicity Wishes, Holly, Polly, Daisy and Winnie had spent most of their Saturday morning queuing for tickets they weren't sure they were ever going to get.

"I'll give up being a fairy if we don't get in!" said Holly dramatically as she looked longingly at the circus poster.

"The acrobats look such daredevils!"

gushed Winnie, staring intently at their costumes.

"It's the clowns I want to see!" giggled Polly.

"I can't wait to watch the performing ponies," said Daisy, stroking their image on the poster.

Felicity raised her eyes to the sky and shook her head. "Oh, Daisy! Ponies are silly! They're not even magical!"

"These ones are!" said Daisy. "They can fly!"

Felicity exchanged knowing looks with Winnie, Holly and Polly. All fairies knew that ponies couldn't fly. The circus ponies were made to look like they could fly with strong harnesses and invisible wires. But none of them wanted to spoil the illusion for their unwitting friend.

"Yes," said Felicity earnestly to Daisy. "I'm sure circus ponies can fly!"

And as she looked up, Felicity saw that the queue had moved on and they were only ten fairies from the front.

* * *

At last the big night arrived. Each of the friends had deliberated for days as to what they were going to wear. The circus was performed in a large and airy big top that was bound to be cold. But Felicity knew that the heat of the excitement generated from so many flapping fairy wings could make it very warm indeed.

Felicity had finally settled on a neat short-sleeved dress, layered with a cardigan and jacket. But even before she had sat down she had removed her jacket. As she took her seat she laid it carefully across her lap.

Acrobats quickly descended from the peak of the big top in a swirling, twirling mist of sparkledust. They leapt and balanced, flew and flipped across the circus ring in ways the fairies had never seen before.

"Look up there!" hissed Holly under her breath as she pointed to the far side of the tent where she could just make out a glittering, wobbling shape hovering above the crowd's heads.

"What is it?" Daisy whispered back.

"It must be part of the performance," said Felicity quietly. "It's getting bigger."

"It looks like one of the acrobats," squinted Holly. "She's on the tightrope!"

And within seconds, all eyes were

fixed, not on the acrobats performing a pyramid in the middle of the ring, but on the single acrobat wobbling hesitantly along the mile-high tightrope… without wings!

Gasps of suspense filled the air as fairies watched unblinking, their hands squeezed tightly together.

"She's going to fall!" cried Felicity, distressed.

"She's wobbling all over the place and there's not even a safety net to catch her!" Polly gasped.

The performing pyramid fairies had stopped what they were doing now and they too were watching fearfully. Slowly and carefully, but without much skill, the tightrope-walking fairy was putting one foot in front of another on a rope that was not much wider than the ribbon in Felicity's hair. Several times she misplaced her footing and was able to balance herself just in time. But as she reached the middle of the rope she stopped dead.

"She's lost her nerve," said Holly, terrified. "She can't go on!"

"Someone will have to go up there and save her," said Polly.

"But just think what that will do to her career and her confidence for ever!" cried Felicity. And, without a second thought, she shouted out as loud as she could, "YOU CAN DO IT! GO ON! YOU CAN DO IT!"

And suddenly every fairy in the circus top was clapping and chanting, "YOU CAN DO IT!" too.

Slowly and dramatically, the fairy on

the tightrope lifted one foot gingerly up into the air to place it in front of her. The audience fell immediately silent, not wanting to distract her. As she brought it down she misjudged its place, and, in what seemed like slow motion, the fairy began to wobble one way and then the other, more and more.

The audience could hardly believe what they were seeing and some had stood up, ready to leap into the air to catch her.

And then suddenly the fairy on the tightrope fell! Felicity and her friends were frozen with fear. They wanted to do something, but found all they could do was stare, mouths open wide, unable to believe what they were seeing.

In a flash, the whole big top was filled with a bright white light! And from nowhere a beautiful, strong and dazzling pony flew with speed so swift it created a breeze.

Within seconds of the fairy falling, the pony had caught her to land on his back. As he brought her carefully down to the ground, the crowd went wild!

Everyone had stood up and was cheering! The pony, in acknowledgement, raised himself up on his hind legs and brayed to the audience. The fallen fairy was safely smiling in wonder and waving with glee.

* * *

After the show, Felicity and her friends still couldn't quite believe what they had seen.

"I told you ponies were the best!" said Daisy.

"You're right," admitted Felicity. "They're not silly at all. I felt sure that pony was looking right at me. He was very clever, and amazingly talented."

"Did you see how the pony's friends gathered round him at the end, as if to congratulate him?" asked Polly.

"I know!" said Felicity. "I hadn't realized until then that ponies had feelings."

"Oh, they're just like us," said Daisy. "They feel things in exactly the same way as we do."

"I'm going to see if I can get a photo of the star pony on my phone," said Felicity, reaching into her jacket pocket.

"Oh!" she said suddenly. "My phone's

not here! It must have fallen out in all the excitement."

"We'll wait here for you if you want to go back," said Polly kindly. "Look," she pointed, "the big top's still lit up."

So Felicity flew as fast as she could back to the big top. It looked so much bigger when empty. Quickly, Felicity found where she had been sitting and got down on her hands and knees to feel about the ground.

"Everyone's gone," said a gruff fairy voice. "I think it's safe to talk."

"That went very well," said a squeakier voice. "I think the audience really believed I was just about to fall."

"Yes," agreed the gruff voice, "good acting on your part and a fantastic, faultless performance from Star."

Felicity froze. Oh, no! The performance was a fix!

"Terrible shame that we're going to have to leave Star and his team behind," said the gruff fairy.

"Are you certain about that?" questioned the squeaky fairy. "You haven't found a way that we can transport them for the Circus World Tour with us?"

"If only ponies could fly!" said the gruff voice.

"You know, Star and his friends are going to be very upset. The circus is their life and they won't have much without it," said the squeaky voice.

Felicity sneaked a quick look at the two fairies so that she could recognize them if she saw them again. She had heard enough. Grabbing her phone, she fluttered out of the tent and back to her friends before she was caught. And what a story she had to tell.

Read the rest of

Emma Thomson's

Felicity Wishes

Perfect Ponies

to find out what Felicity

does to help save the ponies.

If you enjoyed this book, why not try another of these fantastic story collections?

Designer Drama

Star Surprise

Clutter Clean-out

Newspaper Nerves

Enchanted Escape

Whispering Wishes

Friends Forever

Sensational Secrets

Happy Hobbies

Party Pickle

Wand Wishes

Dancing Dreams

13 Spooky Sleepover

14 Fashion Fiasco

15 Pink Paradise

16 Spectacular Skies

17 Dreamy Daisy

18 Perfect Polly

19 Winnie's Wonderland

20 Holly's Hideaway

21 Fairy Fun

22 Starlight Songs

23 Crowning Cure

24 Fairy Fame

Perfect Ponies

Storytelling Stars

Glittering Giveaways

Look out for these four special editions

Summer Sunshine

Holiday Hullabaloo

Christmas Calamity

Winter Wishes

Felicity Wishes shows you how to create
your own sparkling style and make magical treats
in this fabulous mini series. With top tips, magic
recipes, fairy products and shimmery secrets.

Fashion Magic

Hair Magic

Make-up Magic

Beauty Magic

CELEBRATE THE JOYS OF FRIENDSHIP WITH FELICITY WISHES!

Felicity Wishes always tries her best to make her friends dreams comes true.

Write in and tell us about a friend you think should be praised for her generosity, sense of fun, and kindness, and you could see your letter in one of Felicity Wishes' books.

Please send in your letters, including your name and age with a stamped self-addressed envelope to:

Felicity Wishes Friendship Competition
Hodder Children's Books, 338 Euston Road, London NW1 3BH

Australian readers should write to...
Hachette Children's Books
Level 17/207 Kent Street, Sydney, NSW 2000, Australia

New Zealand readers should write to...
Hachette Children's Books
PO Box 100-749 North Shore Mail Centre, Auckland, New Zealand

Closing date is 31st December 2007

ALL ENTRIES MUST BE SIGNED BY A PARENT OR GUARDIAN
TO BE ELIGIBLE ENTRANTS MUST BE UNDER 13 YEARS

For full terms and conditions visit www.felicitywishes.net/terms

Friends of Felicity

Dear Felicity Wishes,

My best friends name is Naomi. She is very funny and we both love your books and magazines. I have just got your new book called Fairy Fun. Your new friend, Winnie, has the same style hair as my friend. My favourite colour is pink, just like you. Does Polly still want to be a Tooth Fairy? And does Holly still want to be a Christmas Fairy? And does Daisy still want to be a Blossom Fairy? You would love my bedroom it is pink, and I have pictures of you and your friends on my walls.

Lots of love, Courtney Smith age 9 XXX

me   Naomi

WOULD YOU LIKE TO BE
'A Friend of Felicity'?

Felicity Wishes has her very own website,
filled with lots of sparkly fairy fun and information
about Felicity Wishes and all her fairy friends.

Just visit:

www.felicitywishes.net

to find out all about
Felicity's books,
sign up to
competitions,
quizzes and
special offers.

And if you want
to show how much
you adore and admire
your friends, you can
even send them a
swish Felicity e-card
for free. It will truly
brighten up their day!